# Ian Beck's
# ALONE
## *in the*
# WOODS

Hippo

*For Lily*

Teddy Bears have such a quiet life,
don't they?

Scholastic Children's Books
Commonwealth House, 1-19 New Oxford Street
London WC1A 1NU, UK
a division of Scholastic Ltd
London ~ New York ~ Toronto ~ Sydney ~ Auckland
Mexico City ~ New Delhi ~ Hong Kong

First published in hardback in the UK by Scholastic Ltd, 2000
First published in paperback in the UK by Scholastic Ltd, 2000
First published as a paperback bind-up in the UK by Scholastic Ltd, 2004
This paperback bind-up edition first published in the UK by Scholastic Ltd, 2005

Copyright © Ian Beck, 2000

ISBN 0 439 95399 5

All rights reserved

Printed in China

2 4 6 8 10 9 7 5 3 1

The right of Ian Beck to be identified as the author and illustrator of this work has been
asserted by him in accordance with the Copyright, Designs and Patents Act, 1988.

It was a perfect Spring day. "Come on," said
Lily. "I want to go on a picnic and fly my kite.
Let's ask Mum."

Lily asked if Teddy could come and, of course, he could. So they gathered up the picnic things and the kites, and set off.

Halfway up the steep hill, Lily asked, "Are we nearly there yet?"
"Not far," said Mum. "We'll be there soon."

At last they reached the top of Windy Hill.

They chose the perfect spot.

They laid out the cloth for the picnic.
Lily set Teddy down under a tree.

"Poor old Teddy," said Lily. "There's none for you, but you don't need a picnic, do you?"

After the picnic Mum said, "Let's fly
a kite. Which one shall we take?"
Lily chose the yellow one.

So Mum and Lily set off, leaving Teddy all alone to guard the picnic.

Suddenly a great gust of wind blew, and
tugged at the red kite. The kite lifted,
and, oh dear, tugged at Teddy.

Teddy bump, bump, bumped along the ground.

He was lifted over some prickly brambles and just missed a cowpat.

As the kite lifted higher and higher, Teddy was dragged through a hedge backwards.

He held on to the kite string with all his might
because he was . . .

. . . flying! High up in the air. Now he was higher than the clouds.

He flew as high as an aeroplane.
"Whee!" waved Teddy.

Higher, higher and higher still, but this
was fun!

Then suddenly the wind dropped, and the kite began to fall down through the clouds.

And Teddy fell with it, faster and faster, lower
and lower, down, down into the woods until . . .

. . . he landed 'plop', into something green and sticky! He heard voices whispering in the bushes.

When he looked up Teddy saw bright
eyes looking at him. He felt frightened.
Teddy was alone in the woods.

Then slowly, out of the shadows they stepped,
first one, then two, three, four, and then more,
and more, and more, Teddy Bears.

"You landed in our best jelly," they said. "Never mind, don't be shy, tuck in, it's a party, it's a . . .

. . . Teddy Bears' picnic."
They feasted on jelly and honey buns and
lemonade, and then they all had a little sleep.

When Teddy woke up, it was getting late.
"How will I get back?" he said.
"Don't worry," said the bears, "we'll help."

And so they did. It took a little while to
get Teddy into the air, after all the jelly
and honey buns.

But after one big heave, the wind lifted him,
above the trees, over the hills, and far away,
all the way back, until . . .

. . . he landed, very gently, with the softest bump, just where he had started.

When Lily and Mum came back, Lily said,
"What a good Bear! You missed all the fun.
Never mind. Come on, time to go home."

Good Night, Lily. Kiss kiss.
And Good Night, Teddy. Sleep tight.
But we know what really happened, don't we?

Good Night, Lily. Kiss kiss.
And Good Night, Teddy. Sleep tight.
But we know what really happened, don't we?

Lily hugged Teddy. "Tonight is a special night," she whispered.

"You missed all the fun today, Teddy," said Lily, "but now it is time for bed."

Lily brought Teddy in from the cold.
"Come on," she said, "let's get you warm."

Soon Teddy was dropped safely home, back on to the window ledge. "I must go," called the voice. "I have much to do . . ."

Teddy snuggled up under a warm blanket in a whizzing sleigh.

After what seemed a very long time,
he heard a kindly voice. "Hop on here and
I'll take you home."

But he was soon lost in the snow.

The frosty wind blew up and it snowed harder
and harder. Teddy began to trudge home.

When he stood up, his paws were cold. He felt
lost and alone. It started to snow again.

And fell flat on his face in the cold snow.

. . . he slid right across.

Wheeeeee . . . eee . . . eee. . . ee . . .

He spotted an icy puddle that looked just right
for sliding on. He ran at top speed and . . .

Then he decided to make a big snow bear and, when he had finished, he gave it his own warm scarf to wear.

He stomped round and round, up and down, making lots of deep crunchy pawprints.

Until he ended upside down against a tree in a
field of fresh snow.

He was snowboarding. It was such
fun that he tried it over and over again.

He lost his balance and whoops! He was sliding
fast down the steep hill!

Teddy took a deep breath in the wonderful
crisp air. He began to explore but his paws
slipped on a plank of wood.

He pulled himself up out of the snow.

Until he landed . . . plomp! . . . head first in a snow drift.

. . . and flew on, far above the houses and trees.

Bump! He slid down a roof!
Boing! He bounced off an icy washing line . . .

Whoosh! Teddy was catapulted high into the cold air.

Before they went out, Mum banged shut the window. She didn't see Teddy sitting out there.

"Poor Teddy." Lily wrapped him in a scarf, and put him on the window ledge, so that he could see the snow. "Be careful now," she said.

"Wrap up nice and warm," said Mum. "But we'd better leave Teddy here, we don't want him to get lost."

After a night of snow, the world was white.
Lily and Teddy looked through the window.
"We must go out and play."

*For Lily*

| WORCESTERSHIRE COUNTY COUNCIL | |
|---|---|
| 806 | |
| Bertrams | 19.03.06 |
| | £6.99 |
| | |

Teddy Bears have such a quiet life,
don't they?

Scholastic Children's Books
Commonwealth House, 1-19 New Oxford Street
London WC1A 1NU, UK
a division of Scholastic Ltd
London ~ New York ~ Toronto ~ Sydney ~ Auckland
Mexico City ~ New Delhi ~ Hong Kong

First published in hardback in the UK by Scholastic Ltd, 1998
First published in paperback in the UK by Scholastic Ltd, 1998
First published as a paperback bind-up in the UK by Scholastic Ltd, 2004
This paperback bind-up edition first published in the UK by Scholastic Ltd, 2005

Copyright © Ian Beck, 1998

ISBN 0 439 95399 5

All rights reserved

Printed in China

2 4 6 8 10 9 7 5 3 1

# Ian Beck's
# LOST
## *in the*
# SNOW

Hippo